Where does the sun go in winter?

Contents

Written by Anna Cowper

Illustrated by Joseph Wilkins

Collins

What's in this book?

Listen and say

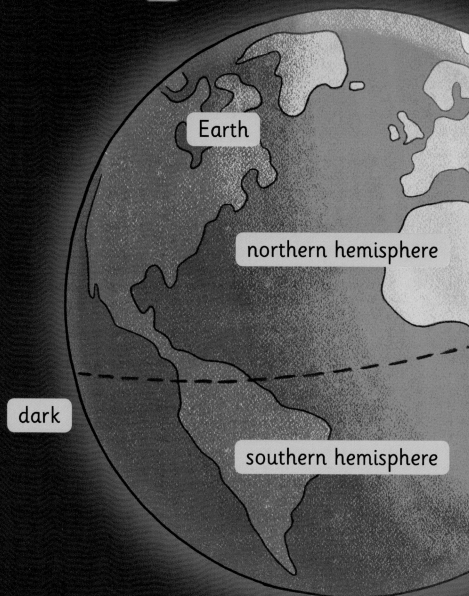

Earth

northern hemisphere

dark

southern hemisphere

sun

light

🎧 This is Birta. She lives in Finland.
In parts of Finland, the winter is very long
and very **dark**.

There is snow on the ground and there is ice on
the lakes.

In December and most of January, the sun never comes up. It's dark all day.

Chapter 1 The Earth and the sun

We get our **light** from the sun. The Earth is always **turning**. It takes 24 hours (one day) for the Earth to turn around.

When the sun is near the part of the Earth where you live, it is the day.

On the other side of the Earth, it is the night.

tilt

The Earth also moves around the sun. It takes 365 days (one year) for the Earth to travel all the way around the sun.

The Earth also **tilts**. When the part of the Earth where you live tilts away from the sun, there is not much light. The days are shorter and the weather is colder. This is winter.

the seasons

spring | summer | autumn | winter

When the part of the Earth where you live tilts to the sun, there is more light. The days are longer and the weather is hotter.
This is summer.

Between summer and winter, it is autumn and between winter and summer, it is spring.

Chapter 2 Winter in Finland

Finland is in the northern hemisphere. It has winter in December, January and February. In the winter, trees and plants do not grow.

Many people are warm inside their houses. Some animals sleep all winter! This is called **hibernating**.

This bear is hibernating.

Chapter 3 Spring

At the end of winter in Finland, it's very exciting to see the sun again!

In our town, we stand and watch the sun come up. We have a big party.

Spring is the season after winter. The weather is hotter. The snow and ice **melt** away.

Plants and flowers start to grow again. There are green leaves on the trees.

Animals stop hibernating and wake up.

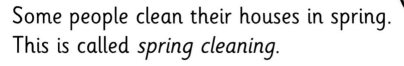

Some people clean their houses in spring.
This is called *spring cleaning*.

There are lots of new baby birds and animals.
Baby birds learn to fly. Other baby animals
learn to walk, swim, jump and find food!

cherry tree

All over the world, people have **festivals** at the start of spring.

In Japan, people go to parks and gardens to enjoy the beautiful flowers on the cherry trees. This festival is called Hanami.

In India, there is a big spring festival called Holi.

People go into the streets and throw **powder** at their friends.

The powder is lots of different colours.

Chapter 4 Summer

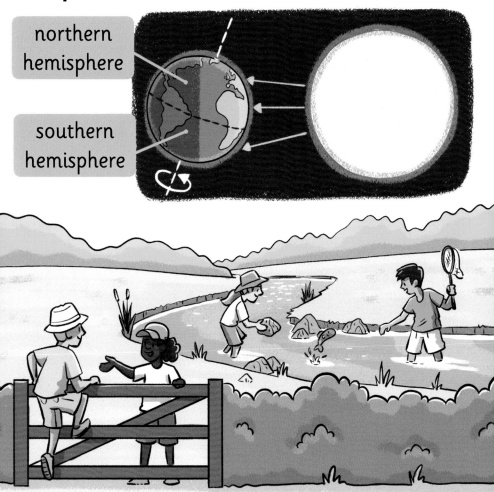

northern hemisphere

southern hemisphere

The season after spring is summer.

The weather is usually hot and sunny.
There's more light and the days are longer.
People enjoy going outside.

Many people have a holiday in the summer.

Many people go swimming in the sea, play on the rocks or walk in the forest.

What do you like doing in the summer?

The places that have the longest
and darkest winters also have the longest
and lightest summers.

In parts of Finland, the sun is in the sky all
night in summer!

It's difficult to sleep.

There are lots of summer festivals.

In Norway, the summer festival starts with a big **fire**.

In Sweden, girls wear white dresses, put flowers in their hair and dance.

In Iran, it's very hot in the summer, so we get up very early.

I play with my friends outside early in the morning before it's too hot!

In the afternoon, we sleep in our houses.

windcatcher

My city is called Yazd. We have tall **windcatchers** on our houses.

The windcatchers catch the wind so our houses are not too hot. In the evening, we sit under them.

In India, we also have very hot summers.

At the end of the summer, there are big **storms** and it rains a lot.

It rains from June to September.

We call this season the monsoon season.

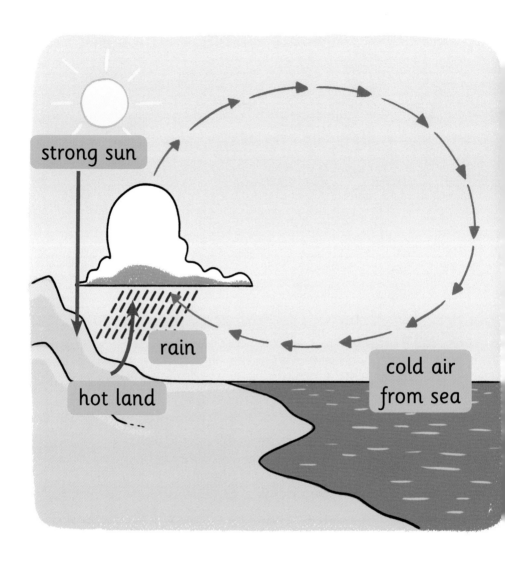

The monsoon is also the name of the wind that brings the rain.

The monsoon winds bring cold air from the sea onto the **land**.

The hot land and the cold air make lots of clouds.

And lots of rain comes from the clouds.

Do you have a monsoon season where you live?

There are lots of festivals in different parts of India when the monsoon starts. People sing, dance and play games.

After the long, hot summer, we're very happy to see the rain.

In many parts of the world, the season after summer is autumn. The leaves on the trees change colour from green to yellow, orange, red and brown.

Then the leaves fall from the trees.

25

The weather is colder in autumn. Animals find food for the winter. Bears eat lots of food because they want to be fat! When they hibernate in the winter, they don't eat for three months!

Farmers are busy in the autumn, too. In the autumn, farmers get the vegetables from the ground and the fruit from the trees.

Chapter 7 Winter and summer!

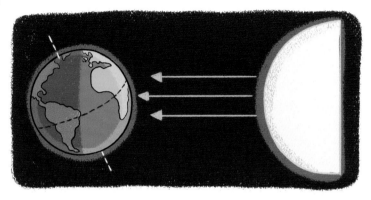

When it is winter in the northern hemisphere, it is summer in the southern hemisphere!

Because the Earth is always turning, the seasons are always changing.

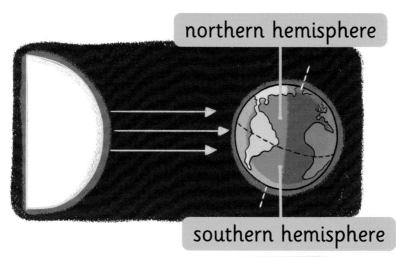

northern hemisphere

southern hemisphere

In many places, there is snow in winter, flowers in the spring and sunny days in the summer. In some places there are monsoon rains and the leaves on the trees change colour in autumn.

The sun never goes away, but the Earth turns and we have seasons.

Mini-dictionary

Listen and read

dark (adjective) When it is **dark**, there is not enough light to see.

farmer (noun) A **farmer** is a person who owns or works on a farm.

festival (noun) A **festival** is a special time when people do something fun together.

fire (noun) A **fire** is a burning pile of wood or coal that you make.

hibernate (verb) **Hibernating** is when some animals sleep through the winter.

land (noun) The **land** is the parts of the Earth where there is no water.

light (adjective) When it is **light**, there is enough light from the sun to see things.

melt (verb) When something **melts**, it changes from a solid to a liquid because it gets hot.

powder (noun) **Powder** is very small pieces of a dry dust, like flour.

storm (noun) A **storm** is very bad weather, when there is heavy rain and strong wind.

tilt (verb) When the Earth **tilts**, it moves round so that one side is higher than the other.

turn (verb) When the Earth **turns**, it moves around in a circle.

windcatcher (noun) A **windcatcher** is a pipe on top of a house that brings wind and cold air into the house in hot places.

1 Look and match

winter

spring

summer

monsoon

autumn

2 Listen and say

Collins

Published by Collins
An imprint of HarperCollins*Publishers*
Westerhill Road
Bishopbriggs
Glasgow
G64 2QT

HarperCollins*Publishers*
Macken House,
39/40 Mayor Street Upper,
Dublin 1
D01 C9W8
Ireland

William Collins' dream of knowledge for all began with the publication of his first book in 1819.

A self-educated mill worker, he not only enriched millions of lives, but also founded a flourishing publishing house. Today, staying true to this spirit, Collins books are packed with inspiration, innovation and practical expertise. They place you at the centre of a world of possibility and give you exactly what you need to explore it.

© HarperCollins*Publishers* Limited 2020

10 9 8 7 6 5 4 3

ISBN 978-0-00-839731-9

Collins® and COBUILD® are registered trademarks of HarperCollins*Publishers* Limited

www.collins.co.uk/elt

British Library Cataloguing in Publication Data

A catalogue record for this publication is available from the British Library.

Author: Anna Cowper
Illustrator: Joseph Wilkins (Beehive)
Series editor: Rebecca Adlard
Commissioning editor: Zoë Clarke
Publishing manager: Lisa Todd
Product managers: Jennifer Hall and Caroline Green
In-house editor: Alma Puts Keren
Project manager: Emily Hooton
Editor: Matthew Hancock
Proofreaders: Natalie Murray and Michael Lamb
Cover designer: Kevin Robbins
Typesetter: 2Hoots Publishing Services Ltd
Audio produced by id audio, London
Reading guide author: Emma Wilkinson
Production controller: Rachel Weaver
Printed and bound in the UK by Pureprint

MIX
Paper | Supporting
responsible forestry
FSC™ C007454

This book is produced from independently certified FSC™ paper to ensure responsible forest management.

For more information visit:
www.harpercollins.co.uk/green

Download the audio for this book and a reading guide for parents and teachers at www.collins.co.uk/839731